Psyche
in a
Dress

FRANCESCA LIA ·BLOCK

Psyche

in a

Dress

JOANNA COTLER BOOKS

An Imprint of HarperCollins*Publishers*

Psyche in a Dress
Copyright © 2006 by Francesca Lia Block

Printed in the United States of America. For information address
HarperCollins Children's Books, a division of HarperCollins Publishers,
1350 Avenue of the Americas, New York, NY 10019.
www.harpercollins.com

Library of Congress Cataloging-in-Publication Data
Block, Francesca Lia.
   Psyche in a dress / by Francesca Lia Block.— 1st ed.
      p.   cm.
   Summary: A young woman, Psyche, searches for her lost love and questions
her true self in a modern retelling of Greek myths.
   ISBN-10: 0-06-076372-8 (trade bdg.) — ISBN-13: 978-0-06-076372-5
(trade bdg.)
   ISBN-10: 0-06-076373-6 (lib. bdg.) — ISBN-13: 978-0-06-076373-2
(lib. bdg.)
   [1. Actors and actresses—Fiction. 2. Psyche (Greek deity)—Fiction.
3. Mythology, Greek—Fiction.] I. Title.
PZ7.B61945Psy 2006   2005017725
[Fic]—dc22

Typography by Neil Swaab
1 2 3 4 5 6 7 8 9 10
❖
First Edition

For Joanna

Weetzie Bat

Cherokee Bat and the Goat Guys

Missing Angel Juan

Girl Goddess #9: Nine Stories

The Hanged Man

Dangerous Angels: The Weetzie Bat Books

I Was a Teenage Fairy

Violet & Claire

The Rose and The Beast

Echo

Guarding the Moon

Wasteland

Goat Girls: Two Weetzie Bat Books

Beautiful Boys: Two Weetzie Bat Books

Necklace of Kisses

Psyche
in a
Dress

P s y c h e

I am not a goddess
I am my father's

My father had me mutilated twice
He had my mother and sisters murdered more than once
but he has never killed me off
sometimes I think he only gave me life
so I could be his muse, his actress

They say he does things with me
to work through issues he had with my mother

I look just like her in the early films but
now she is gone

In the first film I had to take off my top
I stood there, shivering
with my hands covering my breasts
as the cameras were rolling
A million caterpillars crawled over my bones
and my stomach was filled with the wings of dying moths
But I knew what I had to do

I am an actress
I am my father's
I do my job

It was easier after that
I got used to all the crew watching
My father watching
People said that I was odd-looking
not the typical face you see
but my father tells me I am perfect, just what he wants

My father says
"These actors, they try to do too much
You know how to just be
Don't try to do anything else
You are an actress
My princess"

I live with my father
in a dirty-white mansion
made of the bones and teeth of actors
It has been the scene of many atrocities
in my father's films
There are crumbling columns in front
and a dining room we never use
with a giant chandelier from which
one of my father's characters hung herself
There is a huge tiled pool
surrounded by crumbling, headless, limbless statues
ficus trees entwined with morning glories
beds of calla lilies
and oleander bushes

I can see the pool from my window
empty
my father rarely fills it with water
It was used for a drowning in another film
I have a large room
with a large bed draped in diaphanous fabrics
I have my own bathroom with a sunken tub and a view
through glass walls
of my private, somewhat overgrown rose garden
peeling white iron chairs and mossy fountains
I have a walk-in closet of my mother's designer clothes
In one interview I read
my mother said that she sold her soul for that wardrobe
A black satin-trimmed smoking jacket and trousers
a white satin-trimmed smoking jacket and matching satin
skirt, a golden pleated chiffon Grecian gown, a golden
sweater covered with gemstones, a white silk wrap
dress covered with giant red peonies, a pink suit with a
short jacket and skirt, shift dresses in white, black, red
sapphire, emerald and tangerine silk or satin, some
with large bows in back, piles of cashmere sweaters in

lipstick colors, some with silk flowers from obis
appliquéd on them, and many, many shoes

When my mother left us, she took only a black suit
a pair of jeans, a red silk blouse
her jewels and five pairs of the shoes
Sometimes I lie awake at night
wondering how she chose them
I knew which ones they were
because I knew her wardrobe better than she did:
black leather riding boots
black lizard pumps
strappy golden sandals
ruby red flats
emerald green satin dancing shoes with ankle straps
I was so jealous of those shoes
Sometimes I put on one of the dresses
light candles
and dance with my mother's shadow
Most of the time, at night, I use only candles in my room
waiting for her to come back

Even a wraith is better than nothing
even a silhouette on the wall

My father's new girlfriend, Aphrodite
wanted to be the star of his film
and he wouldn't replace me
Once I heard him saying to her, "She's seventeen!
She's seventeen!
What do you expect?"
Enraging her even more
They screamed at each other all night
Until the chandelier shattered
And a thousand swallows flew through the open window
whirring their wings
In the morning she was gone
but she was not finished

One night I was lying in my bed
wearing an antique cotton nightgown
white as a bride
My father was out drinking with his producer
It was completely dark

Not even the candles were lit
I could have been abandoned
on a mountaintop—
the wind in my chest
was that cold
That was when you came
Through the open window
with the night-blooming jasmine
that grows up the old stone garden wall
You knelt beside my bed and put your head near mine
You whispered, "I just want to lie beside you tonight
I won't hurt you"

I was afraid at first
Lay very still, waiting for pain
It felt like a scene from one of my father's movies
The killer with the beautiful voice
For a moment I wondered
if my father had staged the whole thing
If he had a camera somewhere?
I wouldn't put it past him

You only talked to me
You said, "Tell me"
You asked, "Do you think Love and Soul are the same?
If not, how does the Soul earn Love?
How does Love find his Soul?
Can one exist without the other?
If Love and the Soul had a child
what would her name be?"

"Tell me your name," I said
"You already know
If you are Soul
I am the other one"

I heard the sea in your voice—
sheer waves breaking on pale powdered sand
I heard the glossy rustlings of the cypress and olive trees—
the footsteps of maenads and panpipes playing
echoing caves in the mountains—
cloven hooves striking the rock
At their approach birds took flight into the white skies

After a long time I fell asleep

In the morning you were gone

But you came
again and again
I asked to see you but you said
that was the one rule
I couldn't put on
the light
Even so, I asked you to lie beside me
After a while I reached out
and held your hand
"I'm so crazy," I said
"What's wrong with me?
You come through my window at night
I haven't seen your face
And I want you"

Even in darkness
your lips taste of sunshine

They leave a slight stinging spray on my lips
Your skin melts over me
I feel you enter like a shaft of light
My bones dissolve around you
We become liquid, eternal
I am released
from my mortality

You wiped my body with a cool towel
I told you what my father shot today
You said, "If you were my daughter
I would just sit you in front of a camera
and let it watch your face for hours, every expression"
"He cut off my mother's head," I said
"He made it keep talking
She had to have a mask made of her face
plaster and bandages
She is claustrophobic
and she said she almost died
breathing through those little straws"

You held me in your arms
and pressed your lips against my hair
After a long time you whispered
"The wild girls cut off Orpheus's head
He shouldn't have looked behind him
His music could have brought
Eurydice back from the dead"

"But he didn't hear her footsteps," I said

"You can't doubt your gifts"

"Maybe he didn't doubt himself
Maybe he doubted her, his love for her"

You were quiet, thinking

"My father doesn't doubt," I said

"What about you?"

I shook my head
Doubt tastes like sand in the mouth

"Philomela was raped
and her tongue cut out so she wouldn't tell
She turned into a nightingale and sang
her story"

You told me all the myths, one after the other
night after night
my beautiful, brutal bedtime tales
As you spoke I closed my eyes and saw them come to life
the miniature figures acting out their parts
When we fell asleep
my dreams were more vivid than they had ever been
As if I were watching your dreams in my head—

The man who got to be a flower with a hundred petals
admiring himself in a pool forever
while the girl who loved him was only a voice
unable even to choose her words

The girl who crashed through the earth
in a chariot drawn by black steeds
punished for just one red pomegranate seed
unable to choose where she lived
a queen
only in darkness
a princess, her mother's daughter
weaker
in the light

Love's mother, the jealous one
who sent his beloved on a quest
carrying her heart in her hands
like a broken urn
Love the shining god with wings
Love the monster

"I love you," I said
"Please let me
see you"
And you said, "You can't doubt so much, Psyche"

But my half sisters were wearing black dresses
and big sunglasses
Their skin was tan
They came to visit me
I heard their heels click wickedly on the marble floor
"Tell us about this lover of yours"
"There isn't anybody"
"Bullshit," my oldest sister said
"Your skin never looked so good"
They wouldn't stop asking

"I've never seen him," I told them finally
"What?"
They were appalled
"He only comes at night"
"You've never seen his face?"

He smells like night-blooming flowers
Crushed, juicy petals on the pillows
His voice is full of ocean

Humming like the surf
He kneels before me like I am his goddess
He is a god

They laughed at me
Then their faces turned
grave
"You must make him show himself," they said
"He may be a monster"

Why did I listen to them?
They have long white-blonde hair
large breasts
and brown skin
like their mother
I have my mother's black hair, blue eyes and pale skin
full features and large hands like my father
My breasts are small with large aureoles
my legs long and too thin
I know there is something odd

in the way my knees touch and my neck strains
I am not sure why you chose me
Maybe you are a monster?

One night you came to me
I hid in the shadows and waited
I saw a dark figure go to the bed
feel around for the shape of my body
Your movements became more agitated
when you did not find me
You called my name
lay down on the sheets and searched for my scent
moved restlessly for a while like a baby or an animal
and then became
very still
I crept over to you and lit the candle I held
It was a tall taper that smelled of melting honey
In its light my lover was revealed

Is beauty monstrous?
If so, then my sisters were right
His beauty was so sharp it could have cut

out my heart
He lay naked, sleeping on my bed
How could it be?
Why had he chosen me?
I wanted to run and hide from him

As I stood, amazed, a drop of wax from the candle fell
and touched his bare shoulder
He cried out and leapt up
His face filled with pain

"I told you not to look at me," he said
"My mother was right"

No girl wants to hear those words

He was so bright, a conflagration
And I
I had seen too much
I had seen the god
I was not
a goddess

I dropped to my knees and covered my eyes
"Don't come back here," I said

"Why do you doubt so much, Psyche?"

He reached to touch my shoulder but I pulled away
And then he was gone

My room has never been so empty
There is only one monster
Here
She is ready to do anything to be forgiven
She has been mutilated
(On film, but still)
Her mother has been murdered more than once
Now the monster's mother is just gone
What more must monster girl do to find the god again?

E c h o

The film my father put me in was called *Narcissus*
He saw that I was broken
and he thought it might work well for his next project

I went to the set without any makeup
The ladies frowned at my skin
turned my face this way and that
in the harsh lights

"What are you eating?" they asked me
"Dairy? Sugar?"

"Do you get any sleep?"
"Supplements? Facials?"
"You've got to start taking care of yourself"

I shrugged
I said I was okay
I had just inherited my father's complexion
And now of course
I didn't have the benefit of sex with a god every night

At least in this film no one gets raped, mutilated
or murdered
Unless you count vanishing as murder
It's what you assume in this world these days
when someone
disappears
I was supposed to vanish
turn into a voice

Narcissus came to the first reading late
He didn't apologize

My father didn't say anything
Anyone else
he'd have fired on the spot
Instead he just scowled
at me
I turned away so he couldn't see

Narcissus had long, gold ringlets
chiseled features
and a body like a temple
Don't look too deeply into his eyes, though
You will never find your reflection

I'll probably be fine if he doesn't touch me
I told myself
But that was not my father's plan

Narcissus and I went out for dinner
My father set it up
There was a bar of red-veined marble
with spigots spurting wine like blood

Stargazer lilies stained the white linen tablecloths
with their rusty powder
A woman was covertly nibbling the petals
The food had no scent
Beautiful people sat staring at themselves in the mirrors
Their twins emerged out of glass pools
to have sex with them on the tabletops
In the candlelight I wondered
if Narcissus might find me attractive
Not that I cared
Love had already left me

I had on makeup and a blue satin chinoiserie dress
my mother's jewels—
a double strand of pearls and her sapphire ring
I imagined her teeth, her eyes

I asked Narcissus about himself
I didn't expect him to say anything interesting
but when he started talking I fell
under his spell

Instead of touching parts of my mother
I watched Narcissus's full lips move over *his* white teeth
His eyes were pools shattered by sunlight
and his lashes brushed his cheekbones
If he was looking at his reflection
I couldn't see

Narcissus

*N*arcissus lived with his mother in an apartment on a street
lined with other apartments that looked just like it——a cottage
cheese stucco-and-glass building with a pool in the center.

Narcissus swam alone late at night with his reflection. The
pool made everything blue, including Narcissus's skin. The air
always smelled of chlorine. When Narcissus swam it got into his
hair so he washed carefully with his mother's expensive sham-
poo before he went to sleep.

After school, Narcissus took the bus to the beach where he
went surfing or perfected his tan. When he got home his mother
was never there. He defrosted his dinner and went into the

bathroom paneled with mirrors. He took off his clothes and admired his abdominal muscles, his skin, his cock.

Narcissus's father had left before he could remember. His mother was not there. She said she was an actress but Narcissus suspected something else because there were never any roles he knew of but always enough money, heavy makeup, tight dresses, the stink of men. Narcissus never wanted to smell like that.

When he talked to her she looked right through him if she looked his way at all. But suddenly he had discovered, in those mirrors, someone even more beautiful. Someone completely devoted. Someone who would never look away.

A lot of people didn't look away. There were women and men wanting sexual favors. But Narcissus stopped caring about them. It was easier to stand in front of the mirrors, caressing himself.

Sometimes his twin would materialize. Cold as glass and without a smell but so beautiful that it didn't matter. They could fuck all night, tireless, insatiable, exactly the same.

One day on the boardwalk a tall, thin man with pale skin, a hat and dark glasses approached Narcissus. The man seemed out of place and spoke with a thick accent. He handed Narcissus his card and said, "Have you ever acted before?"

Narcissus smiled because in some ways that was all he had ever done. "Why?" he asked.

"I am making a film," the man said. "I need someone to help make my daughter disappear."

"Do you know what I like about you, Echo?"
Narcissus said
"You know how to listen
Most of these actresses I know
just want to go on and on about themselves"

Perhaps this, too, was a test
Narcissus did not taste of the spray
that spurts from the skin of ripe oranges
When we touched it was for the cameras
His pupils were blank

empty

My reflection was never there

The lights were bright, revealing the monsters

He watched himself the whole time

"Who are you?" Narcissus's character asked

"You . . . you . . . you"

Those were my lines

I went home and looked in the giant tarnished mirror

with the frame of silver roses

I had not vanished

I had not faded

away to just a voice

Maybe I wish I had

It was my voice that had been stolen away

E u r y d i c e

Stray dogs followed Orpheus through the streets
feral cats crawled onto his lap
wild parrots flew down to light
upon his shoulders
rolling their eyes in ecstasy
eucalyptus trees swooned when he passed them
jacarandas did a striptease of purple petals

Orpheus tapped the mike
and squinted out into the audience
shifting the weight of his narrow hips

He cleared his throat
but it still sounded like he'd just had a cigarette
He ran his hand through his hair, slicking it back
sang a cappella
with his hands in the back pockets of his jeans
leaning into the microphone as if he were going to go
down on it
then played his guitar
Music can make a man a demigod
especially to a girl who has seen Love
up close
and burned
and lost him
especially to a girl without a voice
I had never understood the expression
about your heart being in your mouth
It beat there, choking me with blood

After the last song he came off the stage
and someone introduced us

I could see the dark roots of his bleached hair
The insomniac circles under his eyes
He had the irises of a mystic
Pale, almost fanatical
His voice was gravelly
His hands were warm with large blue veins
I could hear incantations in his blood
"I've seen your films," he said
"I'd like to talk with you more some time"

The next night we ate avocados, oranges and honey
in Orpheus's candlelit cavern deep in the canyon
I wore strapless pale lace and tulle and lilies in my hair
"Tell me," he said
"Tell me a story"
This in itself was an aphrodisiac
My throat opened like a flower

He listened to the myths
The ones my love once gave me

Orpheus liked their darkness and the violence
and the truth
For me it is the transformation

I was restless, sweating in my dress
"Let's go," I said "Let's go, O"
We ran out into the canyon
Up the hillsides to the street
The sky was bright, hallucinatory, pink
We ran into the neighborhood of rotting mansions
When the sun set we roamed their damp lawns
kissed under the purple trees
There was a pink restaurant with a green awning
We broke inside and explored the shadowy booths
the cobwebs draping the bar
We waltzed on the dance floor with ghosts of dead stars
When the sun rose we ate waffles with whipped cream
in an all-night coffee shop
Sunshine burned through the glass
searing the night off our skins
Back in his cavern, Orpheus sang my myths to me

I imagined that I would stop telling stories
stop acting in my father's films
I would give up my aspirations
I do not need to be an artist, I told myself
I do not need to be a goddess
I will be a woman, a wife, a muse

But this is what I could not give up:
I could not give up myself
And my self had become
the memory of the god who once visited me each night
I could not give up the chance to win him back
How could I win him back if I were happy with another?
It would never happen.
I would need to prove myself, suffer
I would need the god
of hell

O r p h e u s

Orpheus was a musical prodigy. What else, with a name like that? In another place and time his mother might have been a muse of epic poetry, but in this world of separation she was only a woman afraid of poverty and growing old. She took all the money her son made from his first album and bought a small mansion with etched-glass windows, gold columns and a spiked gate. She bought a car and furs and jewels for herself, new breasts. In another place and time, Orpheus's father might have been the sun god, or at least a king, but instead he was a frightened, bankrupt man who never told Orpheus's mother to stop what she was doing.

Orpheus refused to play music for anyone. He locked himself in his room and wrote silent poetry in his journals. He could hear the song of it, his secret. Orpheus's mother knocked on the door, wanting another album, more money for new skin—on her face, another fur coat. That was when he left the fancy house that he had paid for with music. He never spoke to either of his parents again.

Orpheus went wandering through the canyons. He found secret underground passageways, crumbling caverns where he hid, got high, smoked packs of cigarettes. One night he ventured out and played his guitar for the birch trees. They danced in the moonlight, their many dark eyes watching, pale silver skin quivering. In the morning the avocado and citrus trees filled his open palms with fruit. Overblown orange poppies with opiate seeds grew out of the parched dirt. Bees let him reach his bare hands into their hives, scooping out gobs of honey, unstung. Rabbits, squirrels and doves gathered to listen to this new Orpheus, the magician, the mystic, realizing his truth, even in a time without muses, kings or sun gods.

It was hard to live on avocados and oranges, and when the tobacco and pot ran out Orpheus got a job as a bartender in a seedy strip club and sang onstage after hours. The strippers were like birch trees, he found—that silvery and wide-eyed, that susceptible to his charms. He slept with a lot of them. But when he met Eurydice he knew he wanted more. Alone in his cavern, with the insatiable dancing trees awaiting him, he wanted a wife.

When Eurydice left him the maenad came. She wanted more than a husband.

After Orpheus began to doubt
he could not reclaim me

If you are to love, never look back
I should have told him
But what do I know?
I am just as filled with doubt
I am only Eurydice
I am known as Orpheus's
I was never a goddess

My father didn't argue with me when I said I had to leave
He smiled to himself
"Whatever you want, princess
You'll be back in time"

I went away to a new city
and half waited for Orpheus to come for me
To lead me back with his poetry

Dear Orpheus, why did you doubt?
You are an artist
When you sing your words
all the women want your child in their bellies
All the men want to stand where you stand
The god of hell should not intimidate you

Orpheus did not come
Days and days passed
I lived in the tall, cold building
I put on the stray pieces I had brought
from my mother's wardrobe
and walked to school bent under the weight of my books

I sat in the echoing lecture halls
and listened for the poetry hidden
in the professors' words
But I couldn't hear it
I ate but the food had no taste
I drank the alcohol
that was given out every night at the parties
I watched my belly bloat and my face break out
Someone offered me acid
but when I looked out my window
eight flights to the ground below
I knew I couldn't take it
It would have been too easy to jump

I wondered if Orpheus was writing about me
I wondered if I was getting closer to hell

My sister called me and said
"Did you hear? Are you okay?"
"Hear what?" I asked
but I knew it was bad

"You know he was dating that crazy singer?
They were doing heroin.
Something happened. Orpheus is dead."

Love had left again
I had no doubts about hell now
I was all the way there

The Maenad

*T*he maenad's father told her she was stupid, a slut. She took off her clothes and danced in the snow, hoping it would make her skin that perfect, white and untouched. But as soon as she stepped into it, the frost became dirty sludge. Her lips were red bitten blood. The roots of her hair were black like the branches that scratched her arms. She wrote poetry and played her guitar so she wouldn't have to cut herself with something sharper than wood, the fingers of trees. Her guitar spoke and lay in her arms but was not warm. She was only looking for someone to love her.

The maenad went to the big faraway city and formed a band. She threw herself around the stage, whipping her neck, flashing her breasts, bruising her hipbones, spinning until the world whirled away. Oh, obliterating ecstasy. When she opened her eyes she spit into the audience, thinking the boys with the beefy faces were her father.

After the shows she was starving, bloodless. She devoured meat, imagining she was ingesting the flesh of the god of pleasure and pain, becoming one with him, divine. She drank wine, imagining it was that same god's blood, the god of the beautiful and the cruel.

And Orpheus, he was like a limb of that god. When she heard him sing she felt herself changing. When she touched him she felt herself becoming powerful, beautiful, pure. They ate wild narcotic poppies in his cavern while the bees and lovesick birch trees clamored outside; they wanted him as much as she did.

"Don't close your eyes," she wailed.

She didn't want him to leave her, even for a moment. Even in his dreams.

She asked him, "Do you still love that girl?"

He said it was over.

The maenad knew the only way she could be sure was to do something irreversible, terrible, mythic.

And you came
hell god
At a concert downtown
Somewhere dark, I don't remember
The air hissed with sound
The chandeliers were shattering
Black smoke swirled around the stage
I sat on the ground
in the pool
of my mother's old aqua blue taffeta dress

I wore rhinestones on my breasts and on my ears
I wore black gloves with the fingers cut out
black satin pointy-toed stilettos like a wicked bird
Bees swarmed around me, buzzing in my ears
I had a forked tongue and horns and a tail
I saw you and I said, that is the one for me
My hair caught fire

You took me home
It was an old Victorian building
wooden floor painted black—
so shiny, a lake—
no furniture except the low black lacquer bed and table
You kissed me until I passed over
The corpse of my body
was stuffed with black lilies and buzzing bees

I forgot Orpheus, my song
I even forgot my first lover, Love
I stopped wanting anything else in the world

We ran through the city
The air smelled of smoke
Pieces of ash rained down
Some headless mannequins
were lined up on the sidewalk by the trash
You put them in your hearse and took them home
In Chinatown the cloisonné vases
were covered with dust
The animals hung dead in the windows
We ate sticky noodles and pork buns with plum sauce
There was a sign next to a cage of chickens
THESE BIRDS TO EAT NOT FOR PETS
No one looked at us as we ran up and down the hills
The air smelled of burning meat
We were invisible
We were demons
I wanted my mother

I am not a goddess, I said
But you are a god
The god of chaos

The god of hell
Hades, my love

You are a businessman
You own a tattoo parlor
and a clothing store that sells leather clothes, masks
whips and handcuffs
sex toys and porn
You are a club promoter
We went to some kind of old mansion you had found
at the edge of the park
I was wearing my mother's white smoking jacket over her
tight black cocktail dress
and black satin shoes with sharp points
People were standing
around a pool
that you had filled with dry ice
Their drinks were a strange, smoky green
I wondered how absinthe tasted
as I ate my poisonous maraschino cherries
The band was playing in what had once been a ballroom

You had discovered them
They looked like birds of prey
and their music beat past me on dark wings
You had the room filled with chandeliers, broken
like crystallized tears
Thousands and thousands of dried leaves
blew through the corridors
Black hounds guarded the doors
Everyone said you were brilliant
Everyone said you were some kind of genius

We went to a small glass café overlooking the dark water
and drank something I didn't recognize
in the red leather booth
"You are corrupting me, my darling," I said
having another bittersweet sip

I felt my body melting under the table
The waves crashed against the rocks
What if I couldn't get up and leave?
Would you desert me here?

No, you took me home again
You bit me gently, not drawing blood
You fed me pomegranate seeds
I sucked the clear red coating off the sharp white pith
The taste was sweet at first
and then dry as dirt, as bone

"I love you so much that I don't care if I die," I told you
So what if you didn't say it back?
Your hair was always cold against my burning skin, cold
and smelled of smoke
Your skin was always cool and sleek
Hades, my love

Are you just one more task
to bring back the lover I burned with my candle wax?
with the flame of my doubt?

One day after we had eaten oranges in the rare sunlight
I remembered him
the pressure of his lips on my forehead

and at my throat—
making my hot skin feel icy with their burn
The calluses and soft places on his hands
The vibration of his voice in his chest
as he gave me the myths again
I told you the story then, and you said
"He was a monster to do that to you
Did he think he was so much better than you
that you couldn't see him?"

I told you about Orpheus and you said
"Maybe he didn't kill himself
Maybe his girlfriend shot him in the head"

You had different ways to bite
I wondered how much more pressure it would take
to make the blood come

Once we drove all the way back to the city I'm from
We passed the cattle waiting for slaughter
by the side of the highway
The air reeked with fear

You said you grew up on a farm
You saw cows killed
When I asked you to tell me more
about your childhood you just laughed
cranked up
the music and rammed
your foot against the pedal

We didn't stop in the city
but drove all the way through to the border
There were signs along the highway
of silhouetted, running people
holding the hands of their children
like animals, like targets

At the border you turned off the music
smoothed your hair with some water
from the bottle you had gripped between your thighs
You took off your sunglasses and spoke politely
"Yes, Officer, no sir"
No one would have suspected you
No one would have thought, This is Hades himself

In the border town the light was harsh
Dust motes looked as if they were catching on fire
You took my hand and we ran
through the unpaved streets, past the little shops
We bought loads of black leather belts
and cuffs studded with sharp silver
You pulled me down some stairs
into a dark bar where you made me drink tequila
I marveled at the worm saturated with poison
My head was pounding as we emerged
back up into the sun
A lovely girl had a huge tumor in her neck
A man was missing his hand
We found a punk band playing in the dust
The lead singer was a Mexican albino
with tattoos all over his body and shaved head
The band was good, really fast
You gave them your card and spoke to them in Spanish
I was so thirsty
We ate some greasy food and you ordered beers
There was a tiny building that said CASAMIENTOS

and you said we should get married
You laughed
and I felt like the worm in the tequila bottle—
bloated, sick, greenish-white, trapped, in love
That night there were fireworks
You grabbed my hand and we ran through the streets
as the sky exploded
There was panic in your eyes I didn't understand

Maybe I had imagined it
I was wearing my mother's green satin cocktail dress
hemmed short, above my knees
and dusty black cowboy boots
We headed back that night
and slept by the sea in your truck
I vomited on the sand
You carried me into the ocean as the sun rose
"Good for hangovers," you said
I was so cold
I didn't stop shivering for hours after I got out
The sun turned the water to aluminum foil

I was afraid it would all just burn up
anyway

Then suddenly you stopped wanting me
You turned away
You wouldn't touch me
I lay staring at your cold, muscular white back
your blue-black shiny hair
I wondered what I had done wrong—
I had lost weight, so my belly was concave again
I was seeing a dermatologist—
Or maybe I was being selfish
Maybe you had been wounded when you were younger
Maybe you had been damaged and this wasn't about me
at all

I tried to ask you if you had been hurt
"Do you know Philomela?" I asked
"Who?"
"The myth
She was raped by her sister's husband

When she threatened to tell, he cut out her tongue
She turned into a nightingale
She sang her story"

"Do you want to know why we don't have sex?"
you asked
I started to cry and you said
"Not everyone has been molested, okay?
Maybe I just don't want to fuck you anymore.
Have you ever thought of that?"
"Is there something I could do differently?" I asked
"We could try it different ways," I said
You smiled at me
Your incisors sharp
Your eyes were two dark bandages
"I thought you'd never ask, baby," you said

The more punishment, the sooner I will be redeemed?
You had finally earned your name.

H a d e s

ades grew up on a farm in an old red house next to a dilapidated barn. There were cornfields stretching to the horizon; maybe they went on forever. Hades believed they were haunted. The wind in the corn sang strange whispers. Sometimes he'd catch glimpses of emaciated people, thin as scarecrows, with corncob pipes, straw hats, missing teeth, wading shoulder deep through the cornfields. Sometimes he imagined he heard children screaming.

Once at baseball practice he was almost struck by lightning. It hit a tree beside him instead, charred and gnarled it, and he kept imagining his own body ruined like that.

In the winter it was so cold that Hades got frostbite. He had stayed out too late in the snow making angels, not wanting to return home. His father told him he might lose his fingers. He lay in bed trying not to cry, imagining the stumps on his hands.

In the summer Hades was always bathed in sweat from the humidity. His mother screamed at him to bathe. "You stink!" At night he ran through the meadows catching fireflies in jars. Then he took them home and watched them die, the lights snuffed out.

He saw animals born and he saw them slaughtered. Blood was just something that was on your hands all the time. Blood was just another bodily fluid. There were more interesting ones.

When Hades wet his bed at the age of five his mother put him back in diapers. She stuck the pins into him. She kept diapering him until he was twelve years old.

When Hades had an erection his mother locked him in the closet. Sometimes she even beat him. This didn't stop Hades from getting hard. It made him harder in every way.

Hades's father waited for him when he came out of the shower. He commented on the size of Hades's penis. He showed his son his own. There was something odd about the way Hades's father taught him to slaughter a cow. There was some kind of pleasure in it. Sometimes Hades's father would set off fireworks from behind the barn and watch to see his son jump at the noise.

Hades's mother did not like how her husband looked at their son. Because of this she beat Hades even harder. She beat him and locked him in the closet and finally Hades left home.

He had been born an unscarred, sweet-smelling baby with pale down on his head that soon fell out and blue eyes that turned pupil-less black. He had been born loving animals and tractors, getting lost in the lightning bug meadows, lost in the angel-making snow. He had become something else entirely. So he decided to become something else again. He changed his name, he changed the color of his hair, he wore eyeliner and grew his fingernails, changed his skin with ink tattoos of devil girls. He went alone into the desert to set off fireworks to immunize himself to loud sounds. He developed an insatiable appetite for meat, any food that bled, that had once had eyes. He became rich, a businessman. He listened to the loudest music, sought it out, to further immunize himself.

Hades saw Eurydice and plucked her like a flower. He became for her the god of chaos, the god of hell. This was why he wanted her. She was proof of his success, his change.

P e r s e p h o n e

At last, she came for me
I had waited forever

I took the train home from my hell god
It was late morning
My mouth was parched
My skin felt raw
My eyes ached in the sunlight
There were bruises and bite marks
hidden under my clothes
One of my ribs was dislocated

I heard it pop out when Hades took me from behind
and every time I breathed
I felt the scrape of it

I did not think of myself as damaged, as a victim
I saw myself as a woman in love
I had forgotten that this was just maybe another trial
another task I must accomplish
another test

She was waiting for me in the lobby of the building
where I lived
Someone had let her in
She had slept all night on the horrible, scratchy sofa
She had gained weight and she had wrinkles
and she was so beautiful to me
I wanted to jump back inside of her
That was all I could think of

She didn't say anything, she just held me
I wept into her long white linen trench coat

My rib hurt more when I cried but I didn't care
She smelled like wildflowers, and that is not the same
as other flowers but much lighter—
a little acrid and sun-warmed and windy
She wore beautiful Italian shoes and no jewels

We went to the hotel where she was staying
It was a small villa overlooking the city
She ordered room service—
poached eggs under a silver cover, smoked salmon,
fruit and cheese, sparkling water
She made me take a bath
using the tiny bottle of green bath gel
and the soft white washcloth
When I came out
wrapped in the white terry cloth bathrobe
we sat on the bed and ate our meal
I realized how hungry I was

"How did you find me?" I asked her
"Your father"

"You went to him?
I thought you were never going to talk to him again"
"Everything was dying," my mother said
"I was killing it; I couldn't help myself
Without you everything was dead
and I knew I had to see him again
To find you
Anything was worth finding you"
"What did he make you do?" I asked
I knew my father. He didn't do things for free
"Oh, nothing, don't worry, darling," she said
"Eat your eggs"
It was dark in the room
The pale green drapes were drawn closed
The sounds of the city were soft, faraway below us

"Now, who did this to you?"
She put her hand on my rib cage
Her fingers felt so good there, so cool
"What do you mean?"
"I'm not naïve, you know

Remember who I married?
I see all the signs"
I shook my head
"It's not like that"
I didn't want to tell her about Hades
Or even Orpheus
I wanted to tell her about my first lover, Love
The one who never hurt me
He killed me but he never
hurt me
Do you understand?

"I know that you are here with the god of hell," my
mother said calmly. "I know because for me everything
is dying. I want you to come back with me so I can come
back to life. We can live together. You can go to school
there. This place is terrible for you. Look at you."

But it wasn't as simple
as that
What if I returned with her

and left my god of darkness?
Would I ever grow up?
Would I ever pass the test?
Would my first lover be mine again?
No, I would stay
a strange little girl, living with her mother
until they both died in some ritual
holding on to each other
the flowers blooming around them
killing them with beauty

"I can't," I told her
"It's more complicated"
"Let's go out," my mother said
as if she wanted to show me
that the beauty of the world would not destroy me
That it was ours

The sun had come out and the city smelled of flowers
Trees were heavy with pink and white blossoms
The fog lay across the bay where Hades lived
It had not come over the bridge

My mother and I went to a café full of lovely people
We ordered brightly colored Italian sodas
and French pastries
Then we went shopping
The store windows were full of ballerinas
and brides in tulle
My mother bought me a white lace vintage dress
with a full skirt
and pale pink leather boots with sharp heels

We went to the art museum
and looked at the visiting exhibit—
boxes full of weird things
china dolls' heads and hands
tree branches hung with crystal eyeballs
shattered pocket mirrors, a dead bird with one wing
paintings of goddesses that looked like men in drag

We sat beside a fountain and petted a golden retriever pup
Art students had set up their easels to work on the plaza
A clown was juggling
There was a skateboarding couple with dreadlocks

There was a man in a white shirt
with the sleeves rolled up, showing off
his brown forearms
He was reading a poetry book
and he smiled at us—bright teeth—
a toss of brown curls like a god in a painting

It was as if my mother had planned the whole thing
to show me what she could give me

That night my mother wanted to meet Hades
I told her no
We could go out together instead

The movie we saw
followed the lives of a group of children
Every seven years
the filmmaker made a documentary about them
The same children who had seemed so charming
and full of promise
changed

grew fat, sad, strange
I wondered how we keep from spoiling the angels
who come to us
I thought of the men I had known
what they must have been like when they were born
So gentle and small
I wondered if I could ever have children
knowing how I might damage them

Afterward my mother and I ate miso soup
and nightshade vegetable tempura
in a restaurant decorated with purple irises
She told me she still wanted to meet Hades

These mothers, they can be persistent

"It's really not that serious," I said
"I want you to know I don't blame you"
said my mother
"I blame your father
And my father for setting such a bad example"

My mother's father had swallowed her whole
and vomited her back up
My father had become a bull
a swan
a cloud
a shower
of gold
so that he could have sex with other women
It made sense that I would choose Hades
Who else would I choose?

I slept next to my mother
in the smooth, warm bed in the pretty hotel
The sheets smelled of bleach and chocolate
The city twinkled and murmured below us
I slept better than I had in years
But in the morning, over croissants and coffee
my mother asked me again

She said, "I have a small whitewashed house in the
countryside, not far from the sea. I bought it with the

money from the jewels your father gave me. I have
flowers instead of diamonds—they're not doing so well
right now, but you should have seen them! What they
can be! There is a wonderful college; you could go
there. We could drink wine and eat ravioli in the plaza
in the evenings. You should see the art! The men! The
light is rose gold at dawn, like blown glass in the
morning, like watermelon when the sun sets on the
city." She said, "I'm leaving today, I want you to come
with me"

But why should I leave?
My mother had left me
a long time ago
All I knew about her, really
came from the movies I had seen her in
the articles I had read
the smell of her clothes
She had abandoned me to her own hell god, my father
Now she was back, trying to take me away from mine
Why should I leave you?

"I'm not ready," I told her. "I am still with him"
"I want you back"
"But you left me. How can I trust you?"

There were tears in my mother's eyes
but she knew I was right
She left that afternoon
And I went back to hell that night

Whenever I felt pain I imagined that I was one step closer
to finding my lover again
I had completed the tasks of patience
self-denial and self-punishment
earned him this way
But what had I really done?
Given up a demigod of poetry
let myself be fucked by hell himself
Were those things enough?

Still, I told myself, I will keep trying

Until I am too old to want to be immortal

I dropped out of school and stayed with Hades
Every day was the same
I would wake late in the morning and make his coffee
After his shower I would help him to dress
combing his hair, choosing his rings
making sure his black leather pants fit smoothly
buckling his belt
helping him with his boots
When he left to make his rounds
I would do the marketing—
Chinatown for spices and dead chickens
Little Italy for fresh pasta and strings of sausages
The Lebanese market for rosewater and lamb
I spent the rest of the day cleaning Hades's house
polishing the black floors, dusting the artifacts
scrubbing the toilet
and cooking his evening meal
Before Hades came home I made sure I had bathed
put on makeup and a beautiful

dress
We ate together and drank red wine
at either end of the long table
We rarely spoke anymore
After dinner Hades left again
Sometimes he took me with him
to an opening of a club or to hear a new band
I held his hand and was very quiet
Usually I wore a dark lace veil over my face
When we returned home
the sky had turned pale with fog like a bride
Sometimes Hades grabbed me
in the large black bed
and sometimes he fell asleep
without touching me, his face to the wall

This went on for six months
I cannot say I was unhappy
I kept thinking that I was paying some important price
My dreams were full of dark treasures
china dolls' heads and hands, shattered pocket mirrors

a dead bird with one wing

I collected them to my breast
gathering my strength

After a while, I packed my things
and took an airplane to stay with my mother

Demeter lived in a whitewashed cottage
in the green hills above the sea
Every day was the same
I woke at dawn and bathed
helped my mother prepare breakfast—
muesli and fruit and cream
Then we went out into the garden and planted
pulled weeds and watered until the leaves
were emeralds
We went into the village
with cobblestone-paved streets
and bought fresh eggs and opalescent milk
Sometimes we went down to the beach

and swam in the sapphire water
We basked in the sun in giant hats
In the evenings we put on lipstick
and flowered gauze dresses we had made
and went to sit in the cafés
We ate pasta and drank wine
and watched each other glow in the candlelight
Men emerged from their marble prisons
So many speaking statues, perfect stone beauties
but we never went home with them
In the morning we gathered blossoms
that had bloomed overnight
This was the life my mother had bought
with the devil's jewels

I cannot say I was unhappy
But sometimes I would wake at night
in my mother's bed
and the smell of flowers through the window
made me wheeze, gulping for breath

Love, he was not there

Every six months I returned to Hades
Then to Demeter's garden
Back and forth between them aimlessly
I belonged to them
And there was something peaceful about that

So, finally
still seeking some kind of punishment
I went back to the city where my father lived

It is always possible to exchange
one hell god for another

Psyche as a Dress

I hadn't seen my father's girlfriend for so long
I didn't recognize her at first
She was sitting in the front of her shop
fingering her dresses
as if she were touching flesh

There were some gardenias floating in bowls
It was a terribly hot day
and the air conditioner was broken
But Aphrodite never breaks a sweat
Cool as white flowers in a case of glass

I looked around the store
at all the things Aphrodite had made
There were dresses of petals
jackets of butterfly wings
or bird feathers
cloaks of leaves
coats of spiderwebs

Aphrodite and I spoke awhile
I told her that I was looking for work
and she asked about school, why I had left
I talked about Hades
It was hard to resist
confessing to a wide-eyed mother figure
She wasn't disturbed by what I said
I think she even smiled a little
Maybe just appreciating
a good story

"You could work for me," said Aphrodite
You are one of my girls already"
I was still shivering a little

from the smile I thought I'd seen
a glimmer on her lips
like a trace of saliva
But I said yes anyway
That was how I began

I worked at the shop six days a week
I never even took a break
just wolfed down a sandwich in between customers
hiding the greasy paper under the counter
wiping mustard off my fingers
as I jumped up to help people

With the money I made
I was able to move out of my father's house
He hardly noticed
Since I had stopped performing in his films
I just wasn't useful

I rented a tiny one-room guest cottage
nestled away in a canyon

You had to take a steep path up behind the main house
to my miniature door
Morning glory vines grew over the roof
There were amaryllis and blue iris in the garden
Tomato vines and sunflowers
Blue glass wind chimes and a path of tiny stepping-stones
Inside, everything was so small I was always stooped over
There was no closet
so I gave away most of my mother's devil-dresses
washed my lingerie in the garden birdbath
and ate outside off a doll's china tea set
and seashell bowls in a ring of tea lights
When I was uncomfortable
I pretended I was in a storybook

In the evenings after work I hiked through the hills
and picked wildflowers for my hair
Sometimes I went alone to the local pub
and had a beer in the dark
watching the boys play pool
Then I came home to my room

with the claw-foot tub and the single bed
decorated with lace and cloth blossoms
from the ninety-nine-cent store

In this cottage I thought I had escaped my hell god
Maybe I had just found his female counterpart

Some days the shop was full of customers
buying up everything
and then Aphrodite was happy
She took me out after work
and ordered sushi and beers
She promised me a life of glamour, travel
wonderful dresses, any men we wanted

I got drunk and said I didn't want any man except one
"Who is that?" she asked, smiling wickedly
I told her about the god who had once come to my bed
The one I thought was a monster
"Oh, Psyche!" she said
"Is beauty monstrous?
What does that say about me?"

Some days no one came into the shop
and Aphrodite called every hour
to see if I had made a sale
her voice more and more frantic
Finally, she stormed in the door—
a whirlwind of red roses—
and demanded that I clean

I got down on my knees
and scrubbed the floor in my white clothes
while a few customers strayed in
stepping over me in their high-heeled shoes
I dusted the shelves in the back of the store
until I was caked with filth
I sorted through boxes of tiny beads and baubles
blue glass stars, abalone fish, quartz roses
jade teardrops, crystal moons
Aphrodite insisted that I organize them perfectly
without a single mistake
"Look at you!" Aphrodite shrieked
"There on the floor covered in dirt
How do you expect any man to want you

let alone that one?"
She put on a dress made of eucalyptus bark
snakeskin and rabbit fur and went off
to dance at a wedding
While she was gone the ants
crawled in from outside and helped me sort the beads
into their own little boxes
Aphrodite came back at midnight, drunk
"Slave," she said
"Witch"

She turned me into a moth
and shredded my wings to make dresses
But then she needed someone to work for her
so she changed me back
My hair was a little thinner after that
but otherwise I felt all right
She made me into a red rosebush
and plucked all the flowers for her dresses
While she worked she said
"Once I was in love like you

I pricked my finger on a thorn
when I ran to help him
My blood made the white rose red
so pretty
but what's the point?
He died anyway"

When she changed me back
my lips and nipples were paler than before
I guess I am lucky
Some girls never return to their original form

In this town there are a lot of dangerous types
I brought Aphrodite wool from the vicious golden sheep
to make her sweaters
I brought her drinking water
from a pool
guarded by dragons
I even went back to the underworld
to find the beauty cream to keep her young
Hades had a new girlfriend, who manufactured it

She was very sweet, actually
She reminded me of myself when I lived with him
wearing a veil, quiet, insecure
except she had a thriving business
called Deadly Beauty
On my way home to Aphrodite
I stayed at a motel on the coast
There were sea lions on the rocks
coughing their warnings
In the darkness of my room
I opened the jar and touched my little finger
to the pearly surface
patted it on my cheek

I was working at the shop when I got the call
My mother was dead

Before I dropped the phone
I saw the large black butterfly
beating its wings against the window
That was how I fell into an enchanted sleep

Why hadn't I decided to stay with her?
What would have been so bad about that life?
The gardens and the sea and the cafés
Was it only that I was afraid
what others might have thought?
Or had I sacrificed her to my lost lover
as I had sacrificed everything

He was still gone
And I had lost Demeter

I had chosen Aphrodite instead

I walked through my life in this strange trance
My eyes were glazed and my mouth was sealed
I worked at the shop all day and played pool at night
because it seemed like a good pastime
for a zombie in a dress
Even Aphrodite acted concerned
One day she came into the shop and handed me a book
"Read this," she said

It was so like my life
that I wondered if the author knew me

There was no photo
But it said where he lived
In my trance I wrote to him
Sent it to the publisher, never expecting a reply
I said that his book was just like my life
and that I would be in his city
Aphrodite was sending me there
to prepare for a trade show

A few weeks later a letter came

We met in the lobby of the hotel where I was staying
It was a small, romantic place with thick Persian carpets
striped satin chairs
marble and brass counters
flowers everywhere

I sleepwalked down the stairs
wearing Aphrodite's white peony dress

Love was waiting in the shadows
I had found him again

He stepped into a circle of lamplight
and it did not burn him

"I should have known it was you," I said

"You did," said Eros
"I wrote it so you could find me"

We stepped into the evening with hardly a word
It was summer and the sweat popped out on my skin
before I could take a step
The city was deserted this time of year
As I remember, there was no one on the streets
Eros and I walked along, speaking softly
He towered over me
even in my high heels I barely reached his armpit
A summer rain began to fall
misting my hair with a veil of drops
Eros took off his light tweed

jacket and draped it gently over me
His body was very thin but his shoulders were broad

We came to a small restaurant covered
inside and out
with broken bits—teacups, plates, figurines, glass
I wondered who had smashed the mirrors
not fearing bad luck

Eros and I sat across from each other drinking
white wine and eating
grilled salmon, couscous and salad
I couldn't remember having taste buds before
We were the only people there
The food just came to us by itself

"How did you write that book?" I asked him
"It's exactly my life. Have you been following me?"

Eros grinned a crooked smile
It was the first time I had really looked into his face
His head was shaved, laugh lines around his eyes

a nose with a bump, as if it had been broken
He had changed

"Maybe a part of you has been following me, my Soul"

Eros walked me back to my hotel
We shook hands in the lobby
No one was there
I could hear the rain on the glass

I didn't let go of his hand
Instead, I led him up the stairs to my room
He hesitated at the doorway, standing in the dim hallway
There were green cabbage roses on the carpet
faded gold and green striped wallpaper
A cart with some leftover baguettes and mineral water
stood outside someone's door
but no one was there
The only sound was the ice machine down the hall
The city so strangely quiet
Everyone was away, where it was cool and dry
The rain had stopped

"I'm sorry," I said, letting his hand drop

"No, it's not you"

"I shouldn't have assumed anything after so long"

"It's not you . . . I just . . . it's been a hard time"

I nodded and stood on tiptoe to kiss

his cheek without touching him

He steadied me with his hands

They were huge and bony

Most men's hands

are not bigger than mine

"Do you want to come in and talk?"

I turned on the lamp

He sat in the large cream damask chair by the window

The lights from the city shone in, fuzzy with the rain

I sat on the bed

"I would like to stay with you tonight," Eros said

"Just tonight

Then I have to leave"

I could feel my throat closing with tears

But what is real?
Maybe Eros and I stayed a month
a year
Who is to say?
Maybe we are still there now

When our lips touched
our clothes fell away
dissolving from our bodies
the white peony dress scattered its petals on the carpet
underwear disintegrating like cobwebs
Eros lifted me onto his hips
and I wrapped my legs around him as he fell
back into the cream damask chair
we kept falling as if through shifting
clouds
I could feel him inside of me
and that is how I awoke from the sleep of deadly beauty

After, we bathed in a tub that became the sea
with liquid topaz water and a beach of pulverized pearls
and we swam there and made love again

Then we ordered room service at midnight
ate omelets and grapes and bread in our bed
and the bed became an island
—covered with aphrodisiac flowers—
where we slept until late in the morning

Every day
I put on one of the dresses from Aphrodite's sample rack
And we ordered books and films and food
brought to the room
We lay in bed
reading and eating and memorizing each other's bodies
We wrote a play together based on his book
In the evenings we danced on the rose-covered carpet—
our ballroom
It went on like this for a day
a month

a year
I still don't know

I know only
that when Eros finally left I had his child inside of me

That was what made it possible for me to release him
even after the sacrifices I had made
even after waiting for so long

Do you want to know the name of the child
of Love and the Soul?
This is her name:
Her name is Joy

E r o s

*T*he house was built on the side of the hill, so it seemed per-
petually to be sliding off. It was mostly glass so that one could see
wooded hills and smoggy skies from almost every room. Eros's
mother had decorated the house all in purple. There were purple
velvet couches and chairs with purple silk beaded pillows, purple
Persian carpets, giant purple candles and huge natural amethysts
reflecting the light that poured through the windows. There was a
terraced garden that Eros had planted with banks and banks of
lavender, hyacinth, pansies and hydrangea—with pennies buried
at their roots to make them the right color—and little fountains
and statues of Eros's naked mother hidden among the foliage.

Eros was not unhappy. But as he grew older his mother began to suffocate him with her love. She couldn't help it. She had never loved anyone as much as herself before. No one had seemed perfect enough. He was perfect. But he felt as if he couldn't breathe. People acted strangely around him. They saw his face, smelled his skin and hair or touched his hand and something happened to them. It was as if all their senses were coming to life. It was too much for Eros sometimes. All that wanting.

He read the myths and learned that the god of love is not only the son of love and beauty but the son of chaos.

Eros felt empty, as if he had no soul. So he went looking for her.

He didn't have to go far. It was his mother who led him to her.

"My boyfriend's daughter goes to your school," she said. "She's featured in every single damn film. You should introduce yourself."

Psyche was the long-legged girl who kept her head bent as if to hide her face with her black hair. She always seemed so sad. He tried to talk to her but she wouldn't look at him. She hurried past in her odd dresses.

Eros could not help himself. He found out where she lived

95

and he crawled in her window one night. He knew she was the part of him that was missing but he didn't know how to explain it to her. He thought that if she saw him she would send him away. Is beauty monstrous?

His mother said, "I heard that girl I told you about eats boys alive. She likes them really good-looking to feed her ego. Then she dumps them. You're so sensitive, sweetie. It's a beautiful quality. I just don't want you to get hurt."

When his soul finally lit the candle he felt betrayed, but he would have stayed anyway. It was she that sent him away. Afraid that she was not enough.

Eros packed his things and left. He traveled across the country. He shaved his head and ate only rice and vegetables until he lost so much weight that every bone showed. He practiced yoga and chanted. He went to museums and read books and saw films. He did not touch anyone. His skin broke out and he lay in the sun to burn away the red bumps. This left shadowy scars on his cheeks. He was called a freak more than once. Love is freakish to those who fear it. He was beaten up and his nose was broken. Love is a threat.

This was all right with Eros. Eros did not want to be a god.

He wanted to be a man. A writer would be nice, too.

Eros wrote about the girl who was his soul and in this way he felt his soul inside of him. He sent the book to his well-connected mother who sent it to her publisher friend. There was really only one reason Eros wanted the book to be published.

It was like writing a letter and putting it in a bottle and sending it out to sea.

Eros's mother had not told him about her new employee, the girl he had lost.

When he found her again he wanted to stay forever in that hotel room in the deserted city. He never wanted to leave her. But he was afraid that she would leave him. That she still felt she was not enough.

He might have tried, though.

Joy changes everything.

I awaited Joy in our tiny cottage
I made little films for my unborn daughter, little myths
Girls were transformed into flowers, trees and birds
but they always came back—
better singers, more fragrant, full of the earth's power

I stopped working for Aphrodite
I was afraid she might turn me into something
and not turn me back
There were other available slaves and witches to help her
and when you are about to become a mother

you just can't take as many chances

Even so, secretly, I wept for Eros
Part of me wished I had remained a flower
Passive, trembling in the sunshine
closing with the darkness
Waiting for some bee to pollinate me
It would have been easier than being a woman
much easier than being a mother

But I couldn't have stayed with Love
Although he had become a man he was still a god to me
And I?
I was a mere mortal
I was not a goddess

After I gave birth to Joy something changed, though
something I could not have predicted
There in the hospital room
I held her to my breast
and she took my nipple into her mouth

she looked up at me with long, still eyes
too large for her face
her fingers wrapped around mine
there was no one else in the world

Then I knew I could live without Love as a man
I had taken him inside me
and given him back to the world
in the form of a girl

I was hers—
my daughter's—
I was divine

Demeter

They say we turn into our mothers

When my daughter became Persephone
I was Demeter

Just because I had loved Hades
doesn't mean I was prepared
when my child found her own hell god

He had one white eye and his nails and his teeth
were filed to points

Sometimes he wore plastic breasts on his bony chest
or a plastic phallus over leather pants
He wailed about carnage in a raspy voice

This is the one who took her from me

All I can think of is how, when she was a baby
she cried for me all the time
I was the only one she wanted
When I held her I didn't even need my hands
She clung to my neck with her arms
to my waist with her legs like a little animal
She slept in my armpit, her mouth on my nipple all night
It was the only way she would sleep
We woke in each other's sweat
She smelled like little white flowers
and baby soap and me—my milk

I had never been so important
to anyone
I felt as if I could make the world blossom

I had
I had made the world bloom with her

Then he came with his teeth
his nails painted black, his rubber clothes
his one eye behind a white lens like a blind man
He smelled of sulfur
He had a metallic gold limousine
and a driver with white gloves
This is the one who took my daughter away

I remember how we spent our days together
We had picnics with the dolls
on a red-and-white-checked cloth in the garden
ate off their china tea set
the tiny, bitter strawberries that grew in the clay pot
miniature carrots, tomatoes and sprigs of mint
drank homemade lemonade from seashells
We filled the birdbath with rose petals
and watched their reflection on the water
We painted our faces with rainbows

and wore giant heart-shaped rings
and wings
of gauze
We went to the library and read books
about baby animals
searching for their mothers
We sang songs of tiny stars, lambs, cakes
What was I thinking?
That this would be enough for her forever?

My mother had hoped the same thing
She had been wrong

My daughter screamed, "You'd say that about any man.
No one is good enough unless he's exactly like you."
She left the house

I want to believe that he put a spell on her
bit her
drugged her somehow
forcibly carried her away on his black motorcycle
But she went by herself

They broke glasses just to hear them shatter
and tore sheets with their hands
like animals with claws
They stayed up all night watching videos of him
dressed as a schoolgirl
His pieces
were about children killing each other with machine guns
about rape and explosions
bodies falling from burning buildings

People blamed him for inciting more of these things
but she said, "He is just a shy kid who was beaten up in
high school. A poet. He re-created himself to point out
the hypocrisy. He sees the world the way it is. You
pretend none of this exists. You live in a dream."

I wanted my dream
I wanted, more than anything
to make a dream and give it to her
to live in, always
But I didn't try to hide her from the world

She wasn't happy at school so I taught her at home.
I took her to foreign movies, gave her all kinds of
books. I let her wear lipstick and nail polish from the
health food store, although I told her she didn't need it.
I let her go to parties, even. I even let her go to that
performance of his. I wasn't too strict. I didn't cause
this, did I? I just wanted her to be happier than I was.

My own father swallowed me
and then vomited me back up
I blame him for what happened to her
If he had loved us she would never have gone away
with the god of hell
And I would not have needed my Hades
Or maybe it is my fault
I doubted myself
I let her real father go away twice

When she left I sat in the garden and lit a cigarette
smoked half of it and let it drop
thinking I could make a small pyre
a performance piece, almost

But the fire started to spread
After the fire department came
I felt guilty, of course
All those nice, strong men
who risked their lives to help people
Not clean up after some crazy, grieving mother
The ground was scarred and barren
She was gone

I thought, this is how I will repay life
for taking her from me
I will never grow another seedling
I will shrivel up in the darkness
and the flowers all die with me

Then one day I went to see
my daughter's Hades
He lived in a dark palace with iron gates and fierce dogs
A huge bald man let me in
He was smiling to himself, I knew
Smirking
Another mother trying to drag her stray child back home

He didn't think I was anyone to fear
I had not been a goddess before Persephone was born
Now I was a goddess enraged, protecting my child

A slender young man came down the staircase
He spoke softly and asked if I wanted a drink
I fingered the knife in my pocket
had imagined this moment so differently
Facing the hell god, slitting his throat
slaying him, bringing her home in my arms
All my fury at fathers and gods
would make me invincible

Instead I just stood there
looking at him with his soft unwashed hair
his stubbled chin and two blue eyes
like my daughter's eyes

He played the piano for me
a bunch of narcissus, white in a vase
The smell made me swoon, so I steadied myself

He sang of a mother and child
looked up at me, grinning, and said
"I could never put this on an album, though.
Reputations involved here"
She came down the stairs, in his shirt
Her legs so small and bare
When she saw me she looked
as if I were her hell

Then he reached out for her
took her in his arms
folded her up
I remembered
how light she once felt
and warm, perfect, safe

I thought
maybe any man who held her would be
like a hell god to me
maybe I can never
give her up

"I'm sorry," I said. "I'm sorry for coming here"
I let the knife fall from my fingers back into my pocket
I turned and left her there
I knew that I could never bring her back
The child I wanted to bring back with me was gone

It was winter
I took a bath in the claw-foot tub
and put on a white silk kimono with red poppies
I made corn, squash and garbanzo bean soup
on my hot plate
I watched the film I had rented
about a biker poet in a leather jacket
His wife went to the underworld
and he had to battle Death
who was not a man
but a pale woman with long black hair
I looked at myself in the tiny mirror on the door
I was no longer beautiful
I did not look like a former starlet
but I looked like an artist

a director of small, strange films
someone you could tell your story to in a bar
someone who had borne a daughter
(a perfect daughter)
someone who knew about planting
and pyromania
I looked like someone whose father had almost killed her
whose lovers had almost destroyed her
whose mother had tried to save her
had saved her as much as a mother can
whose daughter had saved her by being born
and then left her to save herself

One morning I was sitting in the garden
planning where I would plant the sweet peas
and the tomatoes when the weather changed
I heard someone coming up the hillside
My heart felt the way it did when she was a baby
and I had been away from her for a few hours
maybe she was just napping in the next room
but I hadn't seen her face or heard her voice for a while

and then she came in or called for me
and I would fly to her
needing her so much, missing her so much

I didn't try to touch her
She came and sat next to me on the singed wicker chair
"What happened?" I asked her. "Did he hurt you?"
"No. But I'm afraid he will leave me.
There are so many girls all the time."
"What makes you think he wants any of them?"
"I am not a goddess," she said. "You are."
This is what I told her

I have been young too
I have been Psyche, I have been Echo
I have been Eurydice
I have been Persephone, like you
I thought I was not a goddess
My mother was a goddess
Now I am Demeter, like my mother
Because of you

My Demeter tried to save me from Hades

That man you have is Eros too

I let my Eros, your father, leave

because I didn't think I was enough

But you must remember you are everything

We all are

Psyche means soul

What more is there than that?

Echo never stops her singing

Maybe it was Eurydice's choice to fade away

when Orpheus looked back

so she did not have to return with him

Persephone is a goddess of the bridge between

light and dark, day and night, death and life

P s y c h e

*P*syche finished her film about a young woman's quest. It starred her daughter, Joy, and her daughter's boyfriend, the performance artist. Everyone at the indie festivals loved it. They called it poetry. Psyche thought, if I spend the rest of my life alone, it will be all right. I have my art and I have my daughter back. What more could a woman want? Aging is easier without having to worry about a man.

One day Joy and her boyfriend took Psyche with them to a dance. The room was filled with people flinging their bodies around to live drums in front of an altar covered with stargazer lilies and beeswax candles. Psyche stood alone, motionless in a pale blue sheer chiffon tunic dress covered with sequins that reflected the light. She watched everyone—so young, so abandoned. In the eyes of all the men in the room she was no more visible than Echo to Narcissus. The music had no more power to stop her from getting older than Orpheus had the ability to bring Eurydice back from the dead. She watched her child rolling on the floor, doing backbends and handstands, being lifted into the air.

"Come on, Mom," Joy said, taking her hand.

They danced together for a while and then Joy danced away but Psyche kept moving. It was easier than she had expected. Soon she forgot herself entirely. She forgot that she was probably the oldest woman in the room. She forgot that she hadn't danced in years. (Even then it had been mostly alone in her room with her mother's shadow.) After she had been in motion for a long time Psyche began to feel as if she were sixteen. She wanted to say to all the young women in the room, "When your mothers tell you to love and appreciate your body it isn't just to get you to shut up. They know that when you are old you are going to feel exactly the same way inside that you do now. We try on different dresses, different selves, but our souls are always the same—ongoing, full of light."

As she was thinking this, Psyche closed her eyes. A hand was at her waist. She didn't move but kept swaying to the music, feeling the pressure of the fingertips beneath her rib cage. She remembered how when she was Persephone, Hades had popped a rib out as if trying to get better access to her heart. What would he have done if he had actually held it in his hands? Her breath quickened and her legs lightened. All the blood moved to her chest. But her Hades had not come to claim her.

"Eros," she said.

When she opened her eyes, he was standing there. Had she conjured him with her dancing? He looked older now; his hair was close-shaven, nearly all gray. There was nothing about him that screamed "ancient power of the cosmos, love god, son of Aphrodite, son of Chaos." He was a man, getting older, her daughter's father. He was also her first lover, her secret, her storyteller. And he was a god, yes. But she was a goddess and a storyteller too. A soul in a new dress now.